Let's share our toys.

Please?

THE ORIGINAL DESTRUCTIBLES®

Chew Proof • Rip Proof • Nontoxic • 100% Washable

LET'S BE KIND

MILLIONS OF COPIES SOLD!

EKATERINA TRUKHAN

THE ORIGINAL INDESTRUCTIBLES®

For ages 0 and up!

Books babies can really sink their gums into!

Let's be kind—and share our toys.
Let's be kind—and help around the house.
Let's be kind—and always say "Good night."

Learn your very first manners in a book that's INDESTRUCTIBLE.

DEAR PARENTS: INDESTRUCTIBLES are built for the way babies "read": with their hands and mouths. INDESTRUCTIBLES won't rip or tear and are 100% washable. They're made for baby to hold, grab, chew, pull, and bend.

CHEW ALL THESE AND MORE!

$5.99 US / $7.99 Can.
ISBN 978-1-5235-0987-4

Copyright © 2020 by Indestructibles, LLC. Used under license. Illustrations copyright © 2020 by Ekaterina Trukhan. All rights reserved. Library of Congress Cataloging-in-Publication Data is available.

Workman Kids is an imprint of Workman Publishing, a division of Hachette Book Group, Inc.

The Workman name and logo are registered trademarks of Hachette Book Group, Inc.

Distributed in the United Kingdom by Hachette Book Group, UK, Carmelite House, 50 Victoria Embankment, London EC4Y 0DZ.

Distributed in Europe by Hachette Livre, 58 rue Jean Bleuzen, 92 178 Vanves Cedex, France.

Contact special.markets@hbgusa.com regarding special discounts for bulk purchases.

All INDESTRUCTIBLES books have been safety-tested and meet or exceed ASTM-F963 and CPSIA guidelines.

INDESTRUCTIBLES is a registered trademark of Indestructibles, LLC.

Cover © 2023 Hachette Book Group, Inc.
First Edition February 2020 | 10 9 8
Printed in Shenzhen, China | IMFP

WORKMAN PUBLISHING • Hachette Book Group, Inc., 1290 Avenue of the Americas, New York, NY 10104 • indestructiblesinc.com